ڕێوی و لەق لەق

ـ حیکایەتێکی ئەیسوپ

The Fox and the Crane
- an Aesop's Fable

retold by Dawn Casey

illustrated by Jago

Kurdish translation by Anwar Soltani

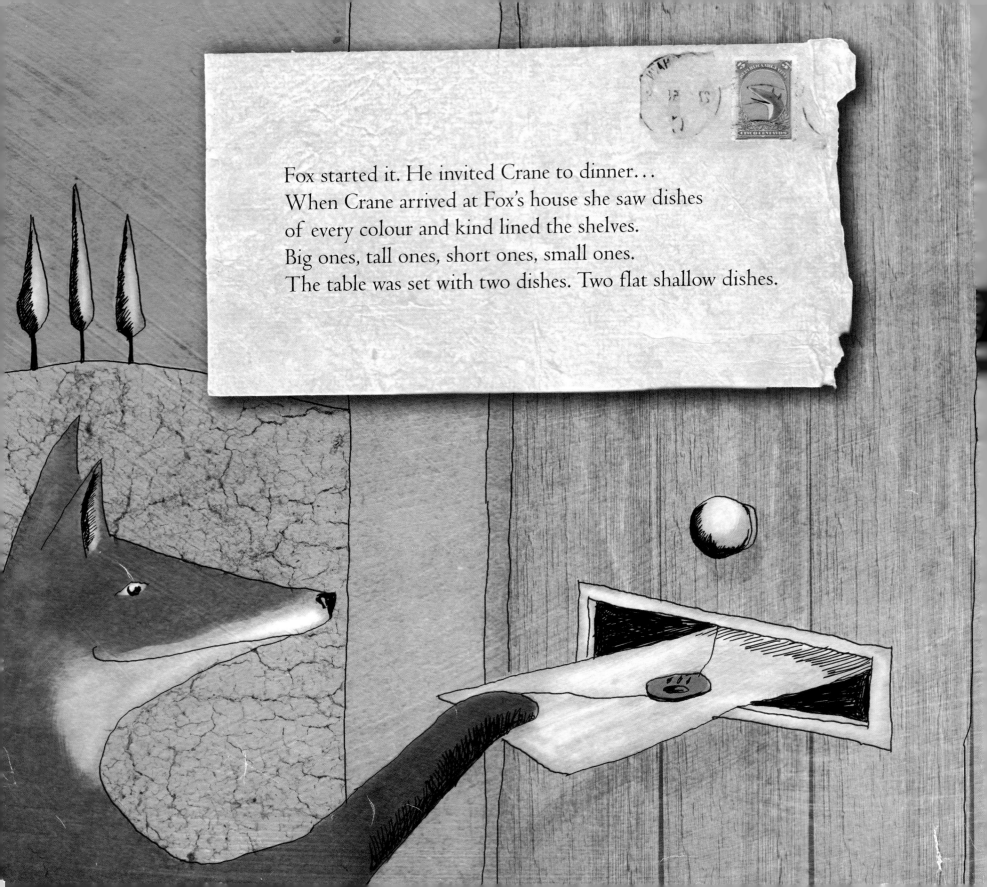

Fox started it. He invited Crane to dinner...
When Crane arrived at Fox's house she saw dishes
of every colour and kind lined the shelves.
Big ones, tall ones, short ones, small ones.
The table was set with two dishes. Two flat shallow dishes.

ڕێوی سەرەتای دامەزراند. لەق لەقی بۆ نانی شێو بانگهێشتن کرد ...

کاتێ لەق لەق گەیشتە ماڵی ڕێوی، سەیری کرد دەفرێکی زۆر لەسەر تافەکان ریز کراون.

دەفری گەورە، درێژ، لەپ، بچووك.

مێزەکەش دوو دەفری لەسەر ئامادە کرابوو. دوانی تەخت و لەپ.

لەق لەق بە دندووکە باریک و درێژەکەی گەلێکی چینە کرد و دەندووکی لێیدا،
بەڵام هەرچی هەرچی کرد و کۆشای نەیتوانی تەنانەت تنۆکێك لە شۆرباوەکە بخواتەوە.

  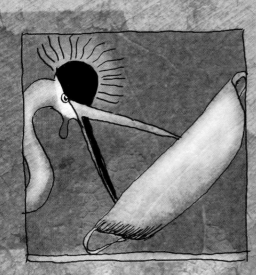

Crane pecked and she picked with her long thin beak. But no matter
how hard she tried she could not get even a sip of the soup.

رێوی سەیری لەقی کرد کە وا توند هەڵەسووڕا و بزەی هاتێ.

ئینجا شۆرباوەکەی بردە سەر لێو و **قوم قوم، شلپەشلپ،**

ملچەملچ هەر هەمووی هەڵلووشی.

پاشان سمێڵەکانی بە پشتەدەستی سرِی و گوتی

"ئاااای چەندە بەتام بوو!"

بە تەوسێکیشەوە گوتی "ئۆی لەق لەق،

خۆ تۆ دەستت لە شۆرباوەکە نەداوە،"

بێ ئەوەش کە پێکەنینەکەی ئاشکرا بکات،

لێی زیاد کرد: "بەداخەوەم کە شۆرباوەکەت

بەدڵ نەبوو."

Fox watched Crane struggling and sniggered.
He lifted his own soup to his lips, and with
a SIP, SLOP, SLURP he lapped it all up.
"Ahhhh, delicious!" he scoffed, wiping his
whiskers with the back of his paw.
"Oh Crane, you haven't touched your soup,"
said Fox with a smirk. "I AM sorry you
didn't like it," he added, trying not to snort
with laughter.

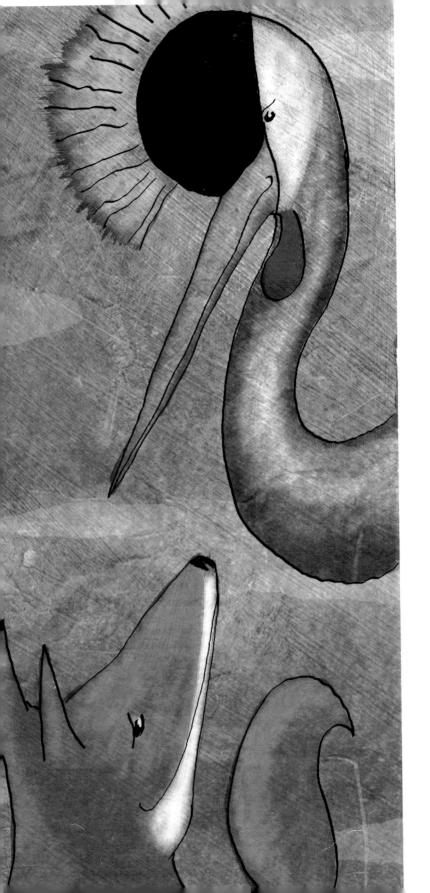

لەق لەق هیچی نەگوت. سەیری خواردنەکەی کرد.
سەیری دەفرەکەی کرد. سەیری ڕێوی کرد
و بزە لەسەرلێو، بەئەدەبەوە گوتی "ڕێوی گیان،
سپاسی میهرەبانییەکەت دەکەم. لێم گەڕێ با قەرەبووی
بکەمەوە ـ تکایە بۆ نانی شێو بێی بۆ مالّی من."

کاتێ ڕێوی گەیشتێ، پەنجەرە ئاوالّە بوو. بۆنێکی خۆشی
لێ دەهاتەدەر. ڕێوی لۆزی هەلّبڕی و بۆنی هەلّمژی.
ئاو چڕایە ناو دەمی، قۆڕەی زگی هات. لچی خۆی لستەوە.

Crane said nothing. She looked at the meal. She looked
at the dish. She looked at Fox, and smiled.
"Dear Fox, thank you for your kindness," said Crane
politely. "Please let me repay you – come to dinner at
my house."

When Fox arrived the window was open. A delicious
smell drifted out. Fox lifted his snout and sniffed. His
mouth watered. His stomach rumbled. He licked his lips.

لەق لەق بە میهرەبانییەوە بالّی بۆ کردەوە
و گوتی "ڕێوی گیان، فەرموو وەرە ژوورەوە."
ڕێوی بەپەلە چوە ژوورێ. لەوێ چاوی بە
چەندەها دەفری هەمەڕەنگ و هەمەچەشن
کەوت کە لەسەر تاقەکان ڕیز کرابوون.
دەفری سوور، شین، کۆن، نوێ.
سەر مێزەکەش بە دوو دانە دەفر ڕازابوەوە.
دوو دەفری درێژ و باریك.

"My dear Fox, do come in," said Crane,
extending her wing graciously.
Fox pushed past. He saw dishes of
every colour and kind lined the shelves.
Red ones, blue ones, old ones, new ones.
The table was set with two dishes.
Two tall narrow dishes.

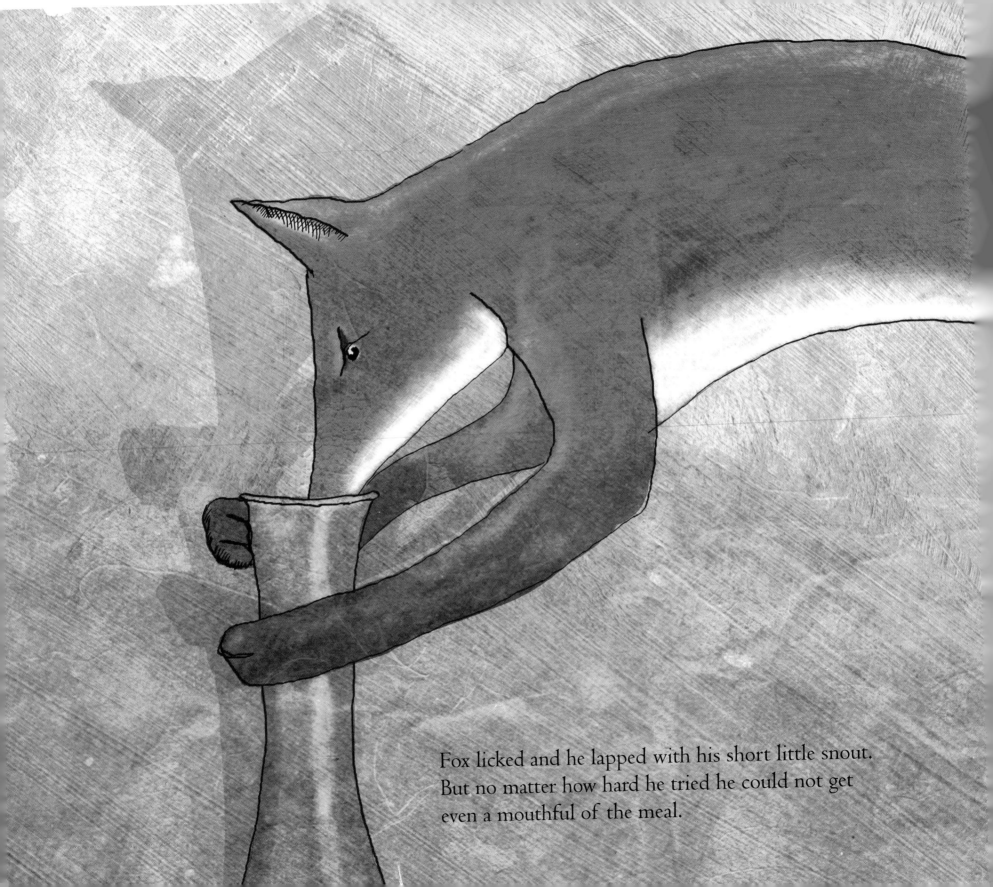

Fox licked and he lapped with his short little snout.
But no matter how hard he tried he could not get
even a mouthful of the meal.

ڕێوی به لۆزی بچووك و كورتی، دهفرهکهی لستهوه
و قهپی پێداکرد. بهڵام ههرچی کردی و کۆشا،
نهیتوانی پڕ بهدهمی خۆی هیچی لێ ههڵقوڕێنێت.

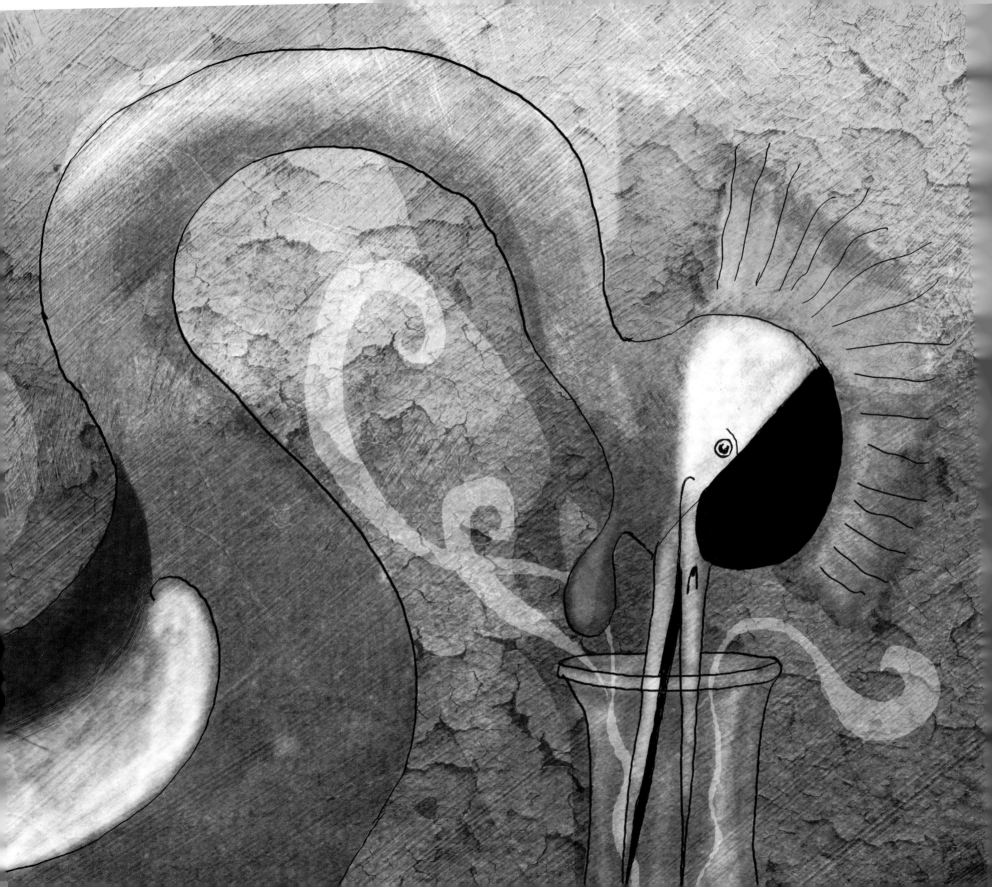

لەق لەق گەلێك لەسەرخۆ چێشتەکەی خۆی دەخوارد و چێژی لە هەموو قومێکی دەبرد.

پاشان بە بزەیەکەوە گوتی "ڕێوی گیان، سپاسی هاتنت دەکەم،

شادمانم کە میهرەبانییەکەتم قەرەبوو کردەوە."

زگی ڕێوی کەوتبوە قۆڕە و هەرا.

تەنانەت کاتێکیش گەیشتەوە مالێ هەر برسی بوو.

Crane ate her meal very slowly, savouring every mouthful.
"Dear Fox, thank you so much for coming," she smiled,
"it has been a pleasure to repay your kindness."

Fox's tummy gurgled and grumbled.
And when he went home, he was still hungry.

The Fox and the Crane

Writing Activity:
Read the story. Explain that we can write our own fable by changing the characters.

Discuss the different animals you could use, bearing in mind what different kinds of dishes they would need! For example, instead of the fox and the crane you could have a tiny mouse and a tall giraffe.

Write an example together as a class, then give the children the opportunity to write their own. Children who need support could be provided with a writing frame.

Art Activity:
Dishes of every colour and kind! Create them from clay, salt dough, play dough… Make them, paint them, decorate them…

Maths Activity:
Provide a variety of vessels: bowls, jugs, vases, mugs… Children can use these to investigate capacity:

Compare the containers and order them from smallest to largest.

Estimate the capacity of each container.

Young children can use non-standard measures e.g. 'about 3 beakers full'.

Check estimates by filling the container with coloured liquid ('soup') or dry lentils.

Older children can use standard measures such as a litre jug, and measure using litres and millilitres. How near were the estimates?

Label each vessel with its capacity.

The King of the Forest

Writing Activity:
Children can write their own fables by changing the setting of this story. Think about what kinds of animals you would find in a different setting. For example how about 'The King of the Arctic' starring an arctic fox and a polar bear!

Storytelling Activity:
Draw a long path down a roll of paper showing the route Fox took through the forest. The children can add their own details, drawing in the various scenes and re-telling the story orally with model animals.

If you are feeling ambitious you could chalk the path onto the playground so that children can act out the story using appropriate noises and movements! (They could even make masks to wear, decorated with feathers, woollen fur, sequin scales etc.)

Music Activity:
Children choose a forest animal. Then select an instrument that will make a sound that matches the way their animal looks and moves. Encourage children to think about musical features such as volume, pitch and rhythm. For example a loud, low, plodding rhythm played on a drum could represent an elephant.

Children perform their animal sounds. Can the class guess the animal?

Children can play their pieces in groups, to create a forest soundscape.

شای دارستان
ـ حیکایەتێکی چینی

The King of the Forest
- A Chinese Fable

retold by Dawn Casey

illustrated by Jago

Kurdish translation by
Anwar Soltani

ریٚوی بەناو دارستاندا دەرۆیشت کە گویٚی لە شتیٚک بوو لەناو گژ و گیادا دەجووڵایەوە .

خشەخش   شتیٚکی گەورە .

چاوترووکاندن   شتیٚک بە چاوی زەردەوە .

بریقە   شتیٚک بە ددانی وەك چەقۆوە .

Fox was walking in the forest when he heard something moving in the long grass.

RUSTLE   Something big.
BLINK   Something with yellow eyes.
FLASH   Something with teeth like knives.

بەور دەمی بە پێکەنین کردەوە. بەو دەمەی کە هیچ نەبوو جگەلە ددان، گوتی "بەیانیت باش ڕێویە بچکۆڵەکە!"
ڕێوی ترسی لێ نیشت.

بەور گوڕاندی و گوتی: "خۆشحاڵم چاوم پێت کەوت، وا خەریك بوو تازە برسیم دەبوو."

ڕێوی دەست بەجێ بیرێکی بە مێشکدا هات و گوتی "چۆن دەوێری! مەگەر نازانی من شای دارستانم؟"

بەور بە پێکەنینەوە نەعرەتەیەکی کێشا و گوتی "تۆ شای دارستان بی؟"

ڕێوی بە شانازییەوە وەڵامی دایەوە و گوتی: "ئەگەر باوەڕ ناکەی بەشوێن مندا وەرە
و بزانە هەموو کەس لێم دەترسێت."

بەور گوتی "دەبێ بە چاو بیبینم."

جا ڕێوی هێدی هێدی بەناو دارستاندا کەوتەڕێ. بەوریش کلکی نابوە سەر نەڕڕەی شانی
و بە شانازییەوە بەشوێنیدا دەڕۆیشت، هەتا ئەوەی ...

"Good morning little fox," Tiger grinned, and his mouth was nothing but teeth.
Fox gulped.
"I am pleased to meet you," Tiger purred. "I was just beginning to feel hungry."
Fox thought fast. "How dare you!" he said. "Don't you know I'm the King of the Forest?"
"You! King of the Forest?" said Tiger, and he roared with laughter.
"If you don't believe me," replied Fox with dignity, "walk behind me and you'll see –
everyone is scared of me."
"This I've got to see," said Tiger.
So Fox strolled through the forest. Tiger followed behind proudly, with his tail held high,
until…

وژ ژ ژ ژ ژ!

بازێکی گەورەی دەندووك خوار! بەڵام هەر ئەوەندەی باز چاوی

بە بەور کەوت، باڵی لێدا و چوه ناو دارەکان.

رێوی گوتی "چاوت لێکرد؟ هەموو کەس لێم دەترسێت!"

بەور گوتی "شتێکی سەیرە!"

ئینجا رێوی خێراخێرا بەناو دارستاندا کەوتەرێ. بەوریش بە کلکی هەندێك

شۆرەوە زۆر لەسەرخۆ بە شوێنیدا دەرۆیشت، هەتا ئەوەی ...

SQUAWK!
A huge hook-beaked hawk! But the hawk took
one look at Tiger and flapped into the trees.
"See?" said Fox. "Everyone is scared of me!"
"Unbelievable!" said Tiger.
Fox strode on through the forest.
Tiger followed behind lightly,
with his tail drooping slightly,
until...

شلپ !

ورچێکی گەورەی ڕەش! بەڵام ورچە هەر ئەوەندەی سەیری بەوری کرد،
کەوتە ناو بنچکە دارەکانەوە.

ڕێوی گوتی "چاوت لێکرد؟ هەموو کەس لێم دەترسێت!"

بەور گوتی "سەرم سوورماوە."

پاشان ڕێوی قورس و قایم بەناو دارستاندا کەوتەرێ. بەوریش لەکاتێکدا کلکی بەسەر
زەوی دارستاندا دەخشا، بەسەری شۆڕەوە کەوتە شوێنی هەتا ئەوەی ...

GROWL!
A big black bear! But the bear took one look
at Tiger and crashed into the bushes.
"See?" said Fox. "Everyone is scared of me!"
"Incredible!" said Tiger.
Fox marched on through the forest. Tiger
followed behind meekly, with his tail
dragging on the forest floor, until…

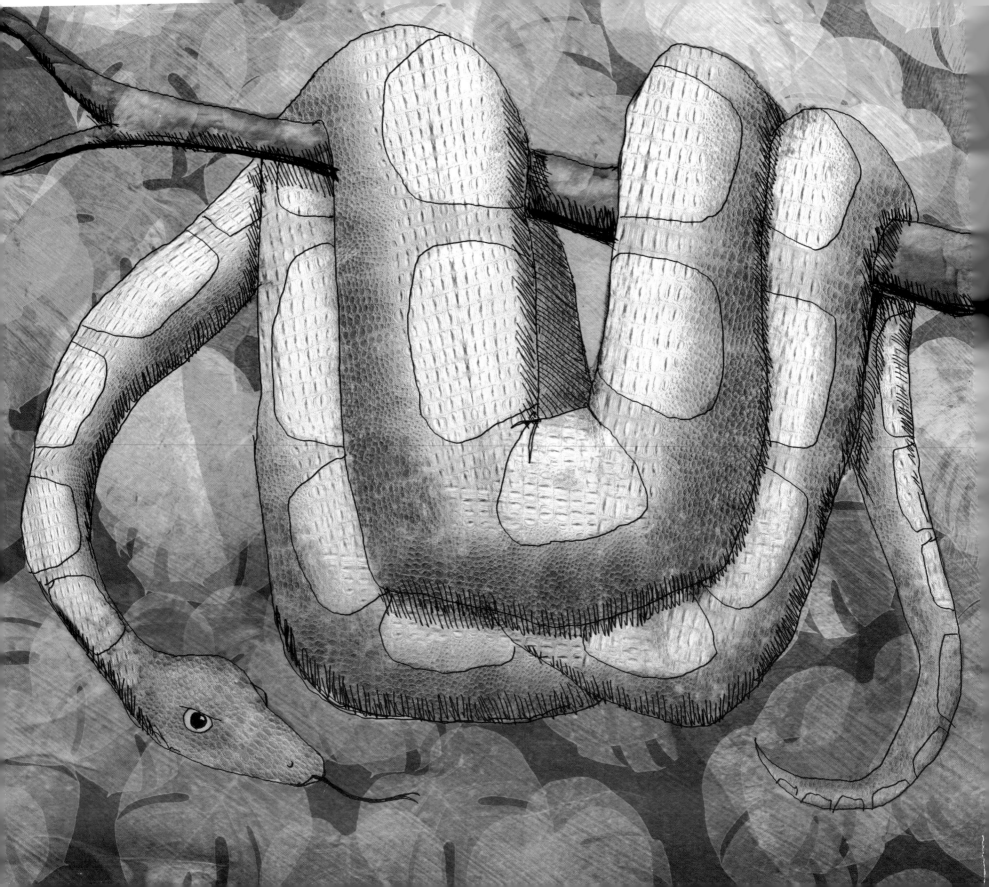

هس س س س س س س !

مارێکی بێ خشپه‌ و دەنگ! بەڵام مارەکه‌ هەر چاوی به‌ بەور کەوت،
خشایه‌ ژێر زه‌وی.

ڕێوی گوتی "چاوت لێکرد؟ هەموو کەس لێم ده‌ترسێت!"

HISSSSSSS!
A slinky slidey snake! But the snake took one look
at Tiger and slithered into the undergrowth.
"SEE?" said Fox. "EVERYONE IS SCARED
OF ME!"

"I do see," said Tiger, "you are the King of the Forest and I am your humble servant."
"Good," said Fox. "Then, be gone!"

And Tiger went, with his tail between his legs.

بەور گوتی "بەڵێ راستە، تۆی شای دارستانی و من خزمەتکاری بەئەمەگی تۆم."

رێوی گوتی: "کەوابوو، برۆ لەبەر چاوم ون بە!"

بەور کلکی خستە ناو گەڵۆزی و بۆی دەرچوو.

ڕێوی، بزە لەسەر لێو، بەخۆی گوت "شای دارستان." بزە بوو بە پێکەنین و پێکەنین بوو بە قاقاکێشان. ڕێوی لە هەموو ڕێگای چوونەوە بۆ ماڵ بەدەنگی بەرز پێدەکەنی.

"King of the Forest," said Fox to himself with a smile. His smile grew into a grin, and his grin grew into a giggle, and Fox laughed out loud all the way home.

To my Nana, with love - DC
For my wife, Alex - J

First published in 2006 by Mantra Lingua Ltd
Global House, 303 Ballards Lane
London N12 8NP
www.mantralingua.com

Text copyright © 2006 Dawn Casey
Illustration copyright © 2006 Jago
Dual language copyright © Mantra Lingua Ltd

A CIP record for this book is available from the British Library